LITTLE MATEY

a make-believe legend of Blackbeard the Pirate's cat

set on Ocracoke Island

by Pat Garber

for the cats of Ocracoke Island

and for all the folks who care for them

with love and kindness

With thanks to those who helped me prepare this book--

Jeannie Griffiths, Betsy Miller, Kevin Duffus,

Connie Leinbach, and Gail Huntley

Big burly black boots were the first sight I had of the man people

 came to know as Blackbeard the

Pirate. I was hiding with my

brother under a canvas tarp in

the stern of our ship. Our

mother had gone down into the

hold to chase down a rat for our

dinner, so we were on our own, playing, when we heard a great commotion—

voices shouting, feet pounding, and a sound like thunder which I came to

know was cannon fire. The ship listed hard to the starboard and we slid out

of our hiding place. My brother crouched back, still out of sight, but the canvas had pushed back away from me, and I was in plain sight, with those

big boots right in front of me.

I heard a booming voice above me and saw, as if in slow motion, a huge

hand coming toward me. Then, quick as lightning, it seized me, entwining me

in its gnarly fingers. There was a noxious

smell, and I thought I was done for. I

tried to bite the dirt-encrusted thumb

that held me down, but it was useless.

Blackbeard swooped me up and, in the

midst of a sword-slashing battle, stuffed

me into a leather sack. He tied it tight and

left me there, on the deck, helpless and trembling with fright, my cries for

help unanswered.

After what

seemed like a terribly

long time I felt myself

hoisted up and jostled

around, then the sound

of water splashing

around me. I heard

that voice again and the sack opened up. The face that peered down at me

was terrible to behold, with raging black hair and beard, piercing black eyes,

and a tooth that flashed gold, but the voice I heard was surprisingly gentle. "Hello, Little Matey," it said, "Welcome to the crew. You're a pirate cat now."

We were on a different ship now, the "Adventure " and the crew included some pretty rough men. Many of them had gold rings in their ears and ugly scars on their faces. Above us waved a flag, which they called the Jolly Roger, with a horned devil and crossbones. It was, I learned, a pirate flag, and I was on a pirate ship.

I thought

about my

brother and

mother and

wondered if I

would ever see

them again. I

was scared to death, but Blackbeard, awful as he looked, treated me kindly.

He gave me a piece of fish to eat, but warned me that I would soon be

expected to feed myself.

He ordered the crew to make sail and, as days passed, I tried to adjust

to my new life. The pirates, my new crewmates, slept on the lower deck, in

hammocks which

swung back and

forth with the

waves. I found a

spot for myself in a

pile of rigging

underneath the

mast. Along with the pirates there lived on the ship a horde of rats, like the

ones my mother used to bring us to eat.

The pirates drank rum which they brought up from Jamaica. I stuck my

tongue in a jug one day when no one was looking, but one taste was all I

needed. It tasted awful! When they weren't tending the lines and sails or attacking merchant ships, my pirate mates liked to play cards or checkers,

and Blackbeard sometimes sat in his cabin reading or writing. Sometimes

they would tell sad

stories, and I would sit

quietly and listen. Some

evenings, when the rum

was flowing freely, one

pirate would pull out a

hornpipe and another a

fife and they would play songs while the rest danced around the deck. Those

evenings sometimes ended in big fights, so I stayed well out of sight.

I soon learned what my duties were. I was charged with catching the big

grey rats that skittered along the ship's beams and down in the hold. I was

young, and some of the rats were as big as I was, so I was afraid of them at first. But when I smelled the moldy biscuits and boiled salt beef the pirates

ate for their dinner, I was quite happy to learn to catch rats and feed

myself. I honed

my skills, and

before too

much time

passed I was

among the best

ratters on the

sea.

One day, after weeks of sailing, Blackbeard, or Edward Teache as he

sometimes called himself, tossed me up on his shoulder and scanned the

horizon. I clung tightly, trying

to ignore the awful smell, and

peered out through the locks

of his black hair. "Land ahoy!"

I heard one of the pirates

shout, "Ocracoke Island!"

I watched as the island

grew larger. I had been in a

seaport once, a terrifying

place that bustled with men and women and strange smells. My mother,

brother and I had hidden below deck while we were there and had only come

out when back on the ocean. This island looked different, however, as we

approached; peaceful, with big twisted trees, a sandy beach, and a sea of

golden grasses that swayed in the breeze. I felt a strange longing to go

ashore and

see what it

was like.

We

anchored

in a quiet

spot near the shore which would one day come to be known as Teache's Hole. Blackbeard and some of his men lowered two boats into the water and rowed to shore. I watched longingly as they scouted around. We stayed at Ocracoke for quite a while, and the men rowed back and forth to the island.

One night I slipped into one of the longboats and hid, and the next morning, when the pirates paddled ashore, I hopped out. This was the first time I'd ever stepped on land, and it was an eerie feeling. At first it was hard to walk straight, and I lurched and stumbled like my mates when they'd had a night of drinking rum. Before long, however, I got my land legs. It felt great to walk on the sandy beach and pretend to chase the little sandpipers which ran ahead of me. I wandered over to a grove of great oak trees and climbed up into the branches, peering down at my mates. I got to wondering

what it would be like to stay here and live on land. When I saw the men getting ready to leave, however, I lost my nerve and slipped back into the boat.

One day a new ship sailed into Teache's Hole.

From the mast waved a flag with a skull and crossbones. It was another pirate ship. It tied up next to us and some of the pirates came aboard. I

was sitting on the boom, watching, when I heard a strange sound. I looked up

and realized it was a cat! Another cat like me, except that I was black, and

this one was grey with stripes. I hadn't seen a cat since I'd left my mother

and brother, and boy

was I excited. I let out

a yowl that just about

got me dropped. "Little

Matey!" Blackbeard

scolded. "What is that

all about?" By then, however, the cat had disappeared out of sight.

Later that evening, when it was quiet on deck, I heard a loud hiss.

Looking over to the other ship I saw the cat sitting in the rigging, grinning at

me. "Hey Sweetheart," he said. "My name is Grog. I'm thinking about jumping

ship here. Want to join me? We could hide out until the pirates leave, and

then have the island to ourselves."

I could feel my eyes grow

wide as I stared at him. I hesitated

a moment before answering. "I'm a

pirate cat, thank you, and my

pirates need me to take care of the

rats." I couldn't sleep, however,

when I tried to take my cat nap. I kept thinking about what he had said and

wondering what it might be like. Sure enough, when I saw a boat setting off

from the new ship the next morning, I caught a glimpse of Grog in the stern.

I'm not sure but I think he

winked at me.

Two days later another ship

sailed in, with more pirates, and

before long they were having a

rollicking party. There were

pirates playing hornpipes and

other pirates joining arms and

dancing around a fire. I saw Grog lurking behind the dunes, watching them.

Then one morning in late November, before the sun had risen, I heard

a shout. I had had a long hard night chasing rats

and I was looking forward to a nice cat nap on

the bow, but I woke up fast. I could just make

out the shape of two sloops in the distance, and

they were heading right for us! Blackbeard

shouted for all hands to prepare for battle.

Before long the roar of cannon fire

boomed and smoke filled the air. I was terrified,

and I started to run and hide in the rigging.

Blackbeard scooped me up, however, before I could get away. "Time for you

to abandon ship,

Little Matey,"

Blackbeard said, and

lifting me up in his

immense hands, he

set me down in a small boat. Then, turning it in the direction of Ocracoke, he

pushed it off. The current seized it and it drifted, with me in it, toward the

island.

That was the last time I saw those big boots or the man they belonged

to. I didn't know what to do when I got to the island, but before long I heard Grog's voice. "Hello Sweetheart," he called, "I'm glad to see you've

finally come to join me!"

He showed me a trail which led to the top of a sand dune, and we watched

from there. The battle raged on for what seemed a long time. I kept

expecting Blackbeard and his men to come rowing back in their longboat, laden with treasure, but they did not return.

Grog invited me to live with him under a pile of brush near the big oaks. I said yes, but I kept looking back toward Teache's Hole, wondering where my pirate mates were and what they were doing. I knew I would miss them, and miss the life of a pirate, but I was intrigued with the idea of living

full time on Ocracoke Island.

The next

spring Grog

and I had a

family, three

darling little

kittens. One

looked like me,

one like Grog, and Little Torty looked like both of us combined.

Now I am a great-great-great grandmother, and my grandchildren are chasing rats all around the island of Ocracoke. So be it next year and the year after and for all the years to come...

Did Blackbeard the Pirate have a cat? Maybe...Was its name Little Matey?

Could have been...Was she the great-great-great-.....grandmother of

Ocracoke's feral cats, often referred to as "Ocracats?" What do you think?

The author, Pat Garber, has always been a bit intrigued with pirates and was, at the age of ten, the captain of her very own "Pat's Pirate Club." She, along with her mates, terrorized the students of Short Pump Elementary School with hand-made pirate hats, cardboard cutlasses, and a pirate flag.

She later became involved in helping homeless cats and was one of the "founding mothers" of Ocracats, Ocracoke Island's feral cat assistance program. The non-profit organization conducts trap-neuter-release clinics, pays for feeding Ocracoke's feral cat colonies, finds homes for kittens, and provides aid and funds for injured or sick feral cats. A portion of the profits from the sale of this book will be donated to Ocracats or other Outer Banks cat rescue organizations.

Pat is the author of *Little Sea Horse and the Story of the Ocracoke Ponies*, a children's book, and *Paws and Tales*, a novel for the young at heart about a cat and a dog on Ocracoke Island. Other books include *Ocracoke Wild, Ocracoke Odyssey, and Heart Like a River.* Her latest book, *The View from the Back of a Whale,* is a collection of poetry and selected prose.

She calls home Ocracoke Island, North Carolina, the Adirondack Mountains of New York, Richmond, Virginia, and the Open Road.

Made in the USA
Middletown, DE
24 April 2019